On the Hill

Lisa Jahn-Clough

Houghton Mifflin Company Boston 2004

Walter Lorraine Books

For my father and his brothers

Walter Lorraine Books

Copyright © 2004 by Lisa Jahn-Clough

www.houghtonmifflinbooks.com

Library of Congress Cataloging-in-Publication Data
Jahn-Clough, Lisa.
On the hill / Lisa Jahn-Clough.
p. cm.
"Walter Lorraine Books."
Summary: Two lonely people, living on opposite sides of a hill, finally
discover each other and fall in love, then must find a way to share
their lives and animals despite their too-small houses.
ISBN 0-618-40741-3
[1. Loneliness—Fiction. 2. Dwellings—Fiction. 3. Animals—Fiction.]
I. Title.
PZ7.J153536On 2004
[E]—dc22
2003014785

Printed in Singapore
TWP 10 9 8 7 6 5 4 3 2 1

On the Hill

Camille lived on one side of the hill.
Franzi lived on the other.

Neither one knew that the other was there.

Camille loved her little house and all of her animals.
But the animals wouldn't dance with her
or carry on interesting conversations.
"I want some company," Camille said.

Franzi loved his little house and all of his animals.
But the animals wouldn't sing with him
or tell him stories at bedtime.
"I want some company," Franzi said.

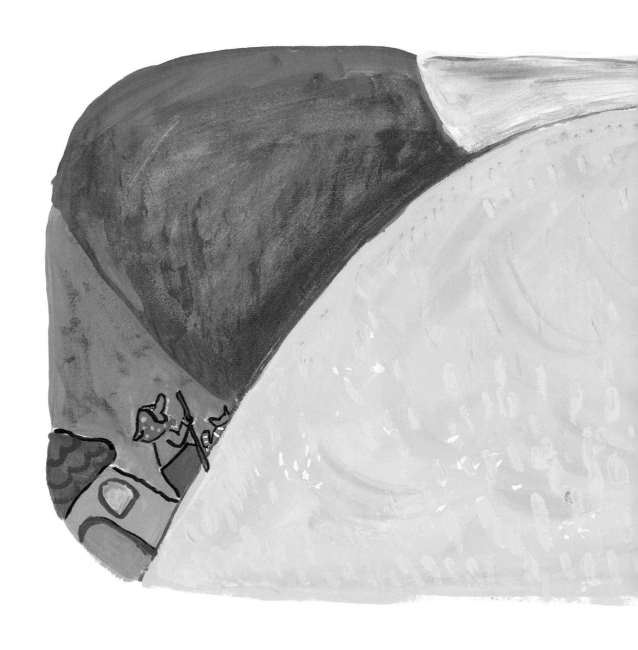

One day Camille went looking for company.
She set off around the hill.

That same day, Franzi went looking for company.
He set off around the hill.

Camille found a house.
"Hello!" she called.
No one was home, except for some cattle.

Franzi found a house.
"Hello!" he called.
No one was home, except for some cats.

Camille went back around the hill to her own house.

Franzi went back around the hill to his own house.

"I still want company," Camille said.
This time she took a different route.

"I still want company," Franzi said.
This time he took a different route.

On the top of the hill Camille ran into Franzi.
"Hello!" they said.

Camille and Franzi told stories and danced for hours.

"Why don't you come to
my house?" Camille asked.
Franzi gathered his animals and
moved into Camille's little house.
But it was too small, and
he missed his own place.

"Why don't you come to
my house?" Franzi asked.
Camille gathered her animals
and moved into Franzi's little house.
But it was too crowded, and
she missed her own place.

Franzi and Camille went back to their own houses.
Something must be done, thought Camille.

This isn't right, thought Franzi.
Franzi and Camille missed each other.

They both ran to the top of the hill.
"What can we do?" asked Franzi.
"I have an idea," Camille said.
She whispered her plan to Franzi.

They went back to their houses and got to work.
Camille took down the walls of her little house.

Franzi took off the roof of his little house.
Bit by bit, they took apart their houses.
They carried the pieces to the top of the hill.

They hammered and pounded
and painted for hours.
Finally they were done.

"Perfect," Camille said.
"It's lovely," Franzi said.

Camille gathered her animals.
Franzi gathered his animals.

And they all lived together
in the house on the hill.

They were happy for ever after.